happy healthy monsters
SQUEAKY CLEAN
(All About Hygiene)

By Kara McMahon
Illustrated by Barry Goldberg

Random House 🏠 New York

ISBN: 0-375-83508-3
Library of Congress Control Number: 2005920822
RANDOM HOUSE and colophon are registered trademarks of Random House, Inc.
MANUFACTURED IN CHINA 10 9 8 7 6 5 4 3
www.sesameworkshop.org
www.sesamestreetbooks.com

A Note to Parents

The basic rules of hygiene are not only the first line of defense against spreading the common cold and the flu bugs that seem to spring up in cycles every year, they are also pretty simple to teach your children! But as you know, hygiene is about more than trying not to get sick during flu season. It's also about being clean and healthy in all ways, and about an overall sense of well-being and comfort.

Incorporating hygiene practices isn't hard, especially if you make it part of your family's daily routine—*and* make it fun for children! Before you know it, these healthy habits can become second nature to the entire family. Kids are naturally curious, and they enjoy learning how to take good care of their bodies.

Here are some basics about . . .

Bathing: Kids should bathe or shower daily. And they should shampoo their hair at least every other day, if not daily.

Hand washing: Encourage your kids to wash their hands often, but e*specially* before every meal and after every trip to the bathroom. Make it a habit for everyone to wash their hands as soon as they come home.

Face washing: Get kids into the habit of washing their faces with soap and water twice a day.

Toothbrushing: Kids need to brush their teeth at least twice a day, once in the morning and always before going to sleep. Ideally, teeth should be brushed after every meal, but even a plain drink of water after eating can help keep teeth clean. Brush gently in circular motions. To make sure that kids brush long enough to get their teeth clean, have them hum the ABC song once or twice through. Also, don't forget to visit the dentist every six months.

Preventing the spread of germs: Remind kids to sneeze and cough away from the direction of others. Encourage them to use a tissue or the inside of their elbow to cover their mouth so their hands stay clean. Teach kids to throw away used tissues, and double-check their pockets at the end of the day just to make sure.

Healing wounds: Explain to your child that it's important to keep cuts and scrapes clean and covered, and that it's also important to dispose of used bandages properly.

We all want Happy Healthy Monsters!

Probably the easiest way to think about keeping your child happy is to imagine a whole pie divided into equal pieces. Think of the pie as your child's day. A child's day, like that pie, should be divided into equal parts so that there is time to rest, which includes getting enough sleep; time to move around; and time to eat three meals a day.

Sometimes the sizes of the pie pieces will change—maybe one day your child gets a lot of time to run around but not an equal amount of time to rest. It happens, but the next day he should get plenty of rest to make up for it. If your child eats a meal that isn't exactly nutritious one day, try to serve two other nutritious meals that day. It's all about trying to even out that pie, or achieving balance.

Ideally, here's what the pie should look like:

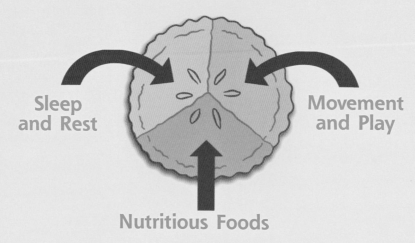

Sleep and Rest

Movement and Play

Nutritious Foods

Sleep and Rest:

You know your child will perform better and feel better if he gets enough sleep. Convincing him of this, however, can be tough. Try to keep bedtime at the same time each night so that it's a set part of the daily schedule. Create a bedtime routine. Reading before bed is a great habit to get into, and it allows him some quiet time to settle down.

During the day you may notice that he needs a nap or some rest time. As he gets older, getting him to take a nap may be hard; still, encourage him to sit down and rest occasionally.

Movement and Play:

Kids need to move, and they need to be encouraged to do so. Stretching, taking a walk, or getting involved in unstructured play are all fine ways for your child to get enough exercise during the day. You don't need to make a trip to a jungle gym— although an outing to the playground is always great. You can create playtime and movement at home by playing Duck, Duck, Goose or Simon Says. Turn on the radio and dance around the room.

If you've ever worked through an aerobics video or sweated through a fitness class, you know that exercise can feel like a chore, but moving can be loads of fun for your child. Find something enjoyable you can do together, such as taking a family walk or bike ride. You'll all benefit from the exercise, and you'll be setting a wonderful precedent for spending time together.

Try making movement a permanent part of your child's day so that it becomes the daily norm. You'll be establishing the basis for him to include exercise in his life in a natural way for all of his life.

Nutritious Foods:

You know green beans are nutritious, but what if your child will only eat hot dogs? Kids can be picky eaters, and they can go through stages when they seem pickier than usual. Don't despair. These are just phases. The best thing you can do for your child is to offer her a variety of healthy foods to choose from. Somewhere amid the green beans, carrots, squash, tomatoes, and Brussels sprouts, she's going to find some vegetable she likes. Don't be shy about introducing different and unusual foods; often a child will be induced by curiosity to try a yam or asparagus or something else new. She'll also notice what you're eating, so eat fruits and vegetables in front of her. Calcium is also an important dietary requirement for growing kids—both boys and girls. Encourage your child to eat yogurt or cheese, and tell her that this will help give her strong bones. If she's not thrilled about drinking milk, try flavored milk—banana or strawberry, for example.

Kids are interested in their growing and changing bodies. Giving them the idea that they can help control how their bodies function by fueling them with certain foods is a great start to a lifetime of healthy food choices.

Some Helpful Hints for
Happy Healthy Monsters

Remember:

⭐ Take a bath every day!

⭐ Use soap and shampoo to keep your body and hair squeaky clean.

⭐ Cover your mouth with your arm or a tissue when you cough or sneeze.

⭐ Wash your hands before every meal, after using the bathroom, and when they're dirty.

⭐ Brush your teeth at least twice a day. Sing or hum the ABC song while you brush.

⭐ When it comes to food, only touch it if you're going to take it.